This Little Hippo
book belongs to

To Kyle and Robbie
B.S.

To my little dreamer Pieterjan.
K.V.

Scholastic Children's Books,
Commonwealth House, 1-19 New Oxford Street,
London WC1A 1NU, UK
a division of Scholastic Ltd

London • New York • Toronto • Sydney • Auckland
Mexico City • New Delhi • Hong Kong

First published in the UK in 2000 by Little Hippo,
an imprint of Scholastic Ltd

Text copyright © Brenda Smith, 2000
Illustrations copyright © Klaas Verplancke, 2000

ISBN 0 439 01351 8

Printed in China

All rights reserved

2 4 6 8 10 9 7 5 3 1

The rights of Brenda Smith and Klaas Verplancke to be identified as
the author and illustrator of this work have been asserted by them
in accordance with the Copyright, Designs and Patents Act, 1988.

GOOD NIGHT, CHARLIE DRAGON!

by
Brenda Smith

Illustrated by
Klaas Verplancke

Little Hippo

It was time for bed on a windy, windy night.
Everyone was asleep . . . except Charlie Dragon.
Charlie tossed and turned. He walked about.
He stretched and yawned. He closed his
eyes tightly but nothing happened.
Charlie went to find his friends
to see if they could help.

"I can't sleep," sighed Charlie. "What should I do?"
"It's easy," said the bats. "Hang upside down like us
and soon you will be fast asleep."
Charlie climbed up to a branch of the tree and hung

upside down just like the bats.
But he was much too heavy.
The branch snapped and Charlie
fell to the ground with a thud!

Bob the Blob crawled to Charlie's side.
"Close your eyes and think of something nice.
You'll be asleep in no time," he said.
"Good idea, Bob," said Charlie.

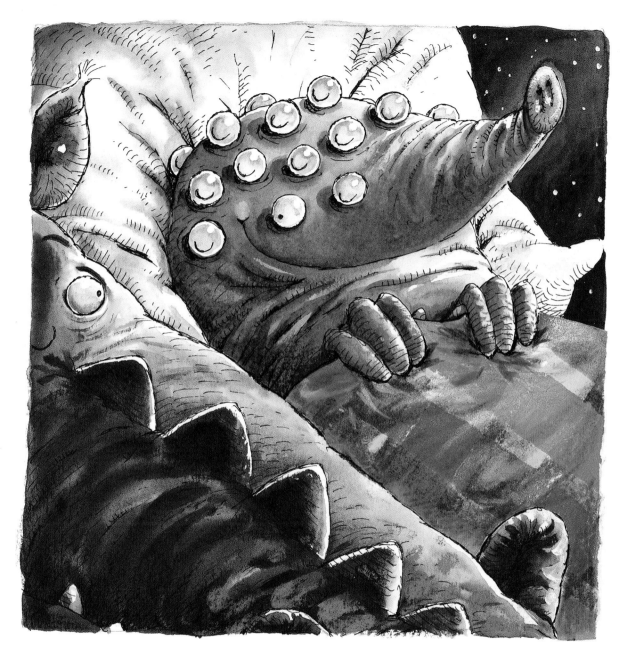

Bob closed his eyes, one by one. Charlie closed his eyes and thought of . . . eating jelly . . . on a beach . . . on a warm, sunny day . . . Bob the Blob started to snore gently. But Charlie Dragon was wide awake.

"Charlie!" shouted the gorillas. "Have a go on our walking machine. You'll soon be worn out!" Sasparilla Gorilla switched the walking machine to **FAST** . . . then to **VERY FAST** . . . . . . then to **VERY VERY FAST**.

"Stop!" cried Charlie Dragon. "I'm so tired, I'm sure
I can go to sleep now. Thank you."
"At last!" cried the other animals. "Peace at last."
Charlie lay down and closed his eyes.
But still he could not sleep.

The wind blew in the trees.
Charlie opened his eyes.
"Don't worry, Charlie," said the birds.
"We'll sing you to sleep."

"Sleep time is here, your friends are near;
Close your eyes tight, we'll sing you good night!"
"What a lovely lullaby," said Charlie. "Thank you.
But I'm still not sleepy!"

Another gust of wind blew over Charlie's head.
"Try counting sheep," said Woolly and Wobbly the
sheep. "Just imagine lots of sheep jumping over a fence,
one by one . . . and count them."

Charlie closed his eyes and imagined sheep jumping
over a fence.
"One, two, three," he counted, "four, five, six . . ."
More sheep. More counting. But it was no good.

Charlie sat up. Everyone else was sleeping happily.
"I can't understand it," he said. "Something's not
quite right." He lay down again and looked up at
the trees. He looked at the birds sleeping peacefully.

He closed his eyes. And then he opened them again
very quickly. "That's it!" he shouted and jumped up.
He had seen something at the top of the tree that
explained everything.

"WAKE UP!" he shouted. **"WAKE UP!**
Cuddles has been blown to the top of that tree."

All his friends looked up. And, sure enough, there was
Charlie Dragon's teddy bear at the very top of the tree.

"Fly up and get him," said Dizzy Tortoise with a yawn.
"Good idea!" said Charlie.
He ran as fast as he could, but he couldn't
get off the ground.

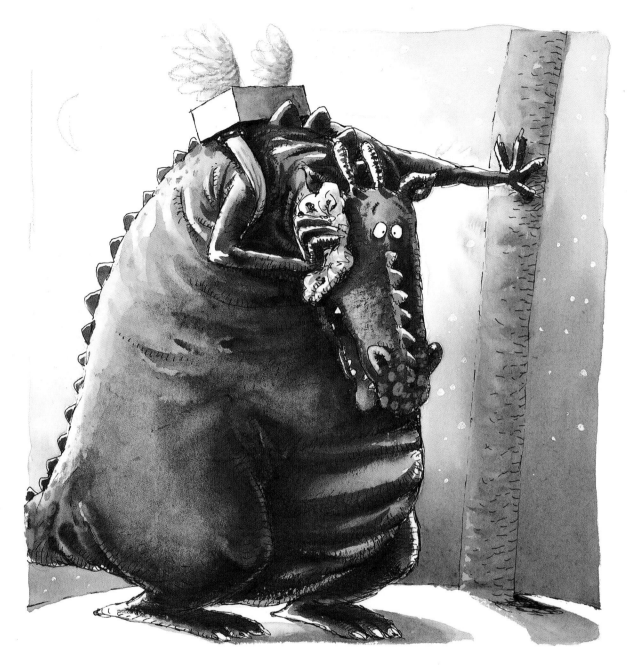

"Oh no!" cried Charlie.
"I am too tired to fly! What can I do?"
All the animals thought hard.

"Try my kite," said Dizzy Tortoise. "It's such a windy night, I'm sure my kite will help you to fly."
"Thanks, Dizzy," said Charlie.

"And I'll lend you my net," said Smiler Crocodile.
"As long as you promise not to break it."
Charlie tied the kite to his back and
carefully took Smiler's net.

Everyone held on tightly to the rope as Charlie Dragon prepared to take off. Charlie took a deep breath.

He ran and ran as fast as he could and this time, with
the help of the kite, he soared high into the air.

At the top of the tree, Charlie stretched and stretched as far as he could. Then he stretched a tiny bit more and Phew! at last he swooped Cuddles safely up in his net.

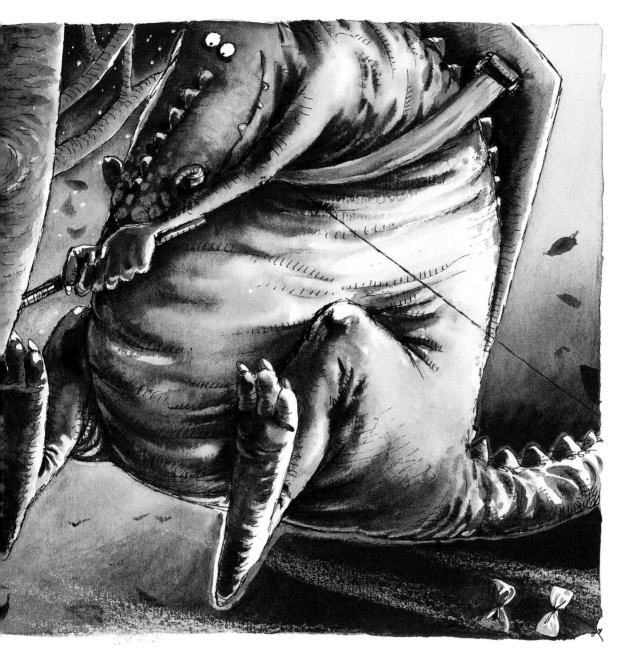

"Hurray!" cried the animals and almost let go
of the rope.

"Cuddles, you're safe," said Charlie, hugging him.

Suddenly, the wind stopped blowing and the night seemed calm.

Charlie and the kite and the net and Cuddles all fell
through the air and landed with a huge, noisy **CRASH!**

But Charlie didn't mind. He was very happy.
"Goodnight, Charlie Dragon," said the animals and
the birds as they crawled back to their beds.

"Goodnight, everyone," said Charlie, smiling.
Then, with Cuddles in his arms, Charlie Dragon yawned
very loudly, closed his eyes and slowly went to . . .

. . . sleep.